THE LAST OF THE MOHICANS

JAMES FENIMORE COOPER
illustrated by N. C. WYETH

A SCRIBNER STORYBOOK CLASSIC
Atheneum Books for Young Readers
New York London Toronto Sydney Singapore

Atheneum Books for Young Readers
An imprint of Simon & Schuster Children's Publishing Division
1230 Avenue of the Americas
New York, New York 10020

Book design by Abelardo Martínez
The text of this book is set in Palatino.
The illustrations are rendered in oil.
Manufactured in China
First Edition
2 4 6 8 10 9 7 5 3 1
Library of Congress Cataloging-in-Publication Data
Cooper, James Fenimore (1789-1851).
The last of the mohicans / James Fenimore Cooper ; illustrated by N. C. Wyeth.—1st ed.
p. cm.—(A Scribner storybook classic)
Summary: An adaptation of the story about the exploits of a young white man
and his Mohican Indian friends during the French and Indian War.
ISBN 0-689-84068-3
[1. Mohegan Indians—Juvenile fiction. 2. Mohegan Indians—Fiction. 3. Indians of North
America—Fiction. 4. United States—History—French and Indian War, 1755-1763—Juvenile
fiction. 5. United States—History—French and Indian War, 1755-1763—Fiction.]
I. Wyeth, N. C. (Newell Convers), 1882-1945, ill. II. Title. III. Series.
PZ7 .C786 Lat 2002
[Fic]—dc21 2001055327

Introduction

For many centuries, the eastern portion of North America was a wilderness of great forests, long rivers, deep lakes, and high mountains. And for centuries the only people who knew the land were the many tribes of Native Americans.

The Native Americans—Indians—respected honor, courage, intelligence, and the pride a man felt from displaying these qualities. When settlers from Europe came to North America, the native people thought these settlers brave and befriended them. The Indians taught the newcomers the ways of their tribes, and how to live in the American wilderness.

A few white men grew to love the way of the Indians and learned to live in the forest with the skill of a native. Settlers no longer, they became rovers, and were called "scouts."

Of all the scouts, Hawkeye was best. Called so by his Indian friends because of his remarkable ability to read the signs of the forest, he was also known as "La Longue Carabine" (French for "The Long Rifle") by his enemies because of his deadly accuracy with his rifle. For many years Hawkeye had roamed the wilderness with his friend, Chingachgook, a noble and wise warrior. As they traveled, Chingachgook raised his son, Uncas, to become a warrior as brave as his father.

In 1754, England and France went to war over the forests and waterways that now separate the United States from Canada. Each army recruited the aid of Indian tribes for their scouting and fighting abilities. The Huron tribe fought for the French. Chingachgook, Uncas, and Hawkeye served as scouts for the English, who were trying to keep the French armies in Canada from expanding southward into the British colonies.

Chapter One

The large buck sprang from the clearing, leapt over a fallen tree, and darted deeper into the forest.

"Look at the size of those antlers," Hawkeye marveled, lowering the front end of his rifle.

"It is truly beautiful," agreed his Indian friend, Chingachgook. "But I do not believe you will down it today. The sun will soon be falling."

"Let us follow him awhile farther," Hawkeye said, tucking his rifle, Killdeer, into the bend of his elbow.

The two began to track the deer farther into the woods. They continued talking, but spoke more softly so that the buck could not hear them.

"You are a great scout, and a great hunter," Chingachgook said. "But you are still only the son of a white man. An Indian no doubt would have killed the animal by now. Why don't you leave the deer to a Mohican?"

Hawkeye knew that Chingachgook spoke of himself. The two friends spoke often of the differences and similarities between Indians and the white man. Hawkeye, dressed in a green hunting jacket, long buckskin trousers, and deerskin moccasins, raised an eyebrow as he leaned closer to his friend.

"Look ye, Chingachgook," Hawkeye said. "Any man knows there is much skill, as well as honor, in the Indian. Yet God has given the white man different senses, different kinds of wisdom. And though their skins are not colored the same, don't they both strive for honor and courage?"

"Some do," agreed Chingachgook. "Some do."

Again they spotted the deer on the crest of a ridge, nearly hidden behind a grouping of trees. They approached slowly.

"Without honor," Hawkeye replied, "a man is nothing but a wild animal or a Huron."

To Hawkeye, Chingachgook seemed to exemplify all that was honorable and noble in man—dignity, intelligence, gravity, beauty, patience, and pride. His shoulders were broad, his back straight, his chest deep. Painted markings of black and white crisscrossed his torso. His head was carefully shaved except for a long, black lock flowing like a horse's tail from the top. His only decoration was the broad feather of an eagle, attached to his topknot and angled across to his left shoulder. A tomahawk and an English knife were stuck in his girdle, and a small English rifle rested across his knee.

"Hawkeye," Chingachgook said, "I do not doubt your honor and courage, but there are white men who want only land and so they steal it from the Indian."

"True," said Hawkeye, "but there are also Indians, such as the Huron tribe, who do not respect truth or honor." As he spoke, he slowly pulled back the flintlock on his rifle with his thumb to prepare to shoot.

The deer, sniffing the wind, sensed that its life was in danger. Again it ran farther from the Indian and the scout.

"Long ago," Chingachgook began, speaking as they chased after the deer, "all Indians were one people, and we were happy. But then the white man came. The white man gave my people the firewater. When my people drank, they foolishly thought that they had found the Great Spirit. They eagerly traded their land for more alcohol. Now I, once a great chief of the Mohicans, have never visited the graves of my fathers because the land now belongs to the white man."

"I know you to be a great chief," Hawkeye said, "but you are without a people." Hawkeye watched a wave of sadness pass over the older man's face.

"You speak the truth, my friend. My people, the Mohicans, have fallen, one by one, to the land of the spirits. I am on a hilltop, Hawkeye, and must go down into the valley; and when Uncas follows in my footsteps to the land of the spirits, there will no longer be any blood of my people on this earth. For my boy Uncas is the last of the Mohicans."

"Do not speak of such sad things," Hawkeye urged him. "We are on the hunt and never is an Indian happier than when he is hunting."

Chingachgook nodded his head in agreement as Hawkeye lifted his long-barreled rifle and began to take aim at the large buck. The animal was grazing behind a bush not far off.

"My friend," continued Hawkeye, "you should think of your son as a young man, not a boy. And someday he will make you very proud as a father."

"Indeed," said Chingachgook, "he will be a great hunter like his father, and all his fathers before him."

"But not as good a hunter as I am," said the smiling Hawkeye, leveling the rifle in the direction of the buck. He began to squeeze the trigger when an arm reached out from behind a tree and knocked the barrel skyward. It was Uncas!

A young Indian in the prime of his youth walked from behind the tree and stood before Hawkeye. Chingachgook smiled, proud that his son was so skillful and quiet that he could surprise even the great Hawkeye in the woods.

"Hawkeye!" Uncas said. "Will you fight the Huron?"

The scout lowered the front end of Killdeer to the earth. The young man was right—the sound of rifle fire would attract any of the crafty Huron warriors that might be in the area.

Chingachgook asked, "Do the vile Huron leave the print of their moccasins in these woods?"

"I have been on their trail," Uncas answered. "They number as many as the fingers of my two hands, but they lie hidden, like cowards."

"The Hurons are thieves, searching for scalps!" said Hawkeye. "They spy for that French general, Montcalm."

"'Tis enough," said the father quietly. "We will chase the Huron from their bushes at sunrise. Let us eat tonight and show the Huron that we are men tomorrow."

Hawkeye pointed toward the deer. "I leave the buck to your arrow," he told Uncas.

The young Indian threw himself on the ground and crept toward the unwitting animal. He fitted an arrow to his bow, and in another instant a twang was heard. Instantly, Uncas leapt up and unsheathed his knife. Moments later, the wounded deer plunged from the bushes and fell at the young Indian's feet.

"'Twas done with skill!" said Hawkeye.

"Huh!" replied Uncas. He bent down to the ground, but rather than attending to the deer, he pressed his ear nearly to the earth. "The horses of white men are coming! Hawkeye, the whites are your brothers; speak to them."

The wounded deer plunged from the bushes.

Chapter Two

Hawkeye stood and cradled his rifle in the crook of his arm as Uncas and Chingachgook slipped behind some bushes. "Who comes?" he demanded as a group of approaching travelers came into view.

"We who have journeyed since sunrise and are sadly tired. I am Major Duncan Heyward," the man on the lead stallion said. "I am English, as are the two women in my charge, Cora and Alice Munro. They are the daughters of the commander of Fort William Henry. That is where we are headed."

Hawkeye looked him up and down, yet said nothing.

"A singer of religious psalms by the name of David Gamut also rides with us," Duncan continued, shifting his weight in the saddle. "We expected to be at Fort William Henry by this very noon."

Hawkeye squinted at the sky, noting the time to be closer to dusk than noon. "You are, then, lost," he said.

"We trusted an Indian guide by the name of Magua to take us to the fort," Duncan told him.

"An Indian lost in the woods!" Hawkeye exclaimed, shaking his head doubtfully. "I would like to look at this creature." He stepped past Duncan's stallion and nodded at the singing-master behind the major.

"David Gamut, singer of fine Christian psalms, at your service," the gangly man introduced himself, removing his hat.

Hawkeye brushed by without a word and moved down the trail to the two girls who sat upon handsome Narragansett horses. The younger of the two had fair golden curls and bright blue eyes that peeked out from beneath her green riding veil.

"I am Alice," the younger girl said with a smile. "And this is my sister, Cora." As fair and light as Alice was, Cora was dark. Her hair was shining and black, like the plumage of a raven. And her eyes were brown and her skin darker than that of her sister.

Hawkeye smiled kindly and asked, "Ladies, where is your guide?"

"He lingers behind," Alice said. She shuddered. "Truth be told, I do not like him."

Hawkeye looked farther down the path. The guide, Magua, was leaning against a tree. He returned Hawkeye's gaze with a dark and haughty look.

Satisfied, Hawkeye returned to Duncan.

"A Huron!" he told the major, once more shaking his head in disgust. "They are a devilish race. I'm surprised he has not already led you to more of his kind."

"Do you think so?" Duncan asked, leaning forward in his saddle. He dropped his voice to a whisper. "I confess I have had my own suspicions."

"'Tis a safe thing to count on the knavery of a Huron," warned the scout. "I will show you the way to Fort William Henry. The woods at night are full of out-lying Huron, and your guide knows too well where to find them." He made a gesture with his hand, and Chingachgook and Uncas slipped from the bushes and came to his side. He spoke to them quickly, then said to Duncan, "Go back to the Huron and hold him in talk. My Mohican friends will sneak round and capture him from behind."

Duncan slowly rode to the rear and found Magua sitting sullenly against the tree.

The Indian stared intently at Duncan as he asked, "Is he alone?"

"Alone?" Duncan answered hesitantly.

Magua sensed his nervousness and slowly, silently, raised himself to his feet. "Then Le Renard Subtil will go," he said.

"Which Frenchman calls you 'The Clever Fox'?"

"'Tis the name the Canada fathers have given to Magua," he said, his voice full of pride.

To give the scout and his companions time to make their approach, Duncan pressed on. "And what will Magua tell the chief of William Henry regarding his daughters? Will he dare to admit to the hot-blooded Scotsman that his children are left without a guide, though Magua promised to be one?"

The Indian did not reply immediately. Instead he looked away from Duncan and examined the forest around him. At last he said, "I have already suffered under the Scotsman once, but Le Renard will not feel his wrath again."

Duncan, noting the Indian's growing tenseness, carefully removed one of his feet from its stirrup. At the same time, he slowly reached toward the bearskin covering of his holsters.

Magua saw the movement and plunged, in a single bound, into the opposite thicket. At the next instant, Chingachgook leapt from the bushes in swift pursuit. Next followed the shout of Uncas and then the woods echoed with the sharp crack of Hawkeye's rifle.

Chapter Three

Hawkeye, Chingachgook, and Uncas were soon back, but without Magua. Duncan looked at them incredulously. "Why didn't you pursue him further? We are not safe while he is free!" he exclaimed.

"He would draw you within the swing of his comrades' tomahawks," Hawkeye told him. He was certain Magua was already searching out other Huron in the forest, and they would return with tomahawks that thirsted for blood. "Come, we must leave here, or our scalps will be drying in the wind this hour tomorrow."

Chingachgook and Uncas took the lead, hurrying the party through the woods. Behind them rode Duncan, the two sisters, and Gamut, whose way of responding to the emergency was to loudly hail God in hymn. Hawkeye, hushing Gamut, kept guard from the rear as they cut through the forest. Once they reached a rocky river, they abandoned the horses for a canoe.

"Water leaves no trail," Hawkeye explained as he helped them into the canoe and pushed it from the riverbank.

The current was swift, drawing them into a series of rapids. The sisters were scared to even breathe, fearing the slightest movement would cause the canoe to pitch and toss them into roiling white water. Hawkeye and his Indian companions struggled to keep the canoe upright, paddling with all their strength until at last, the canoe came to rest upon a flat rock.

"Where are we?" Duncan demanded as they scrambled from the vessel.

Hawkeye pointed toward two boulders tilting over the crashing waters of a waterfall. "There is a cave between those rocks where we can hide for the night," he answered. As Chingachgook and Uncas vanished into the top of the rocks, Hawkeye urged the others to follow.

As darkness fell, Duncan, Gamut, Cora, and Alice entered into a wide, tall cave with dry walls and a dirt floor. Hawkeye and the two Mohicans kept watch outside, but from time to time the scout returned to bring the travelers water and dried meat. Duncan lay down a soft layer of sassafras branches for the sisters to rest upon, and they sat down gratefully. Alice thanked him, then asked, "Do you think our father is worried that we are lost in this wilderness?"

"He is a father," Duncan answered, "and it is in a father's nature to worry about his children."

Alice swallowed tears. She turned to her sister and said, "We have been selfish, Cora, in wanting to see our father with so much danger in the forest!"

Cora took Alice's hand and assured her, "Father is a soldier, and soldiers take chances. He would understand the chance we took in traveling to see him."

Duncan had just taken up Alice's other hand when a horrible cry filled the air. It came from outside. A long, breathless silence followed, then suddenly Hawkeye stepped into the cave. They stared at him, hoping to learn from the expression on his face whether he knew if the noise was made by a Huron.

"Are we in danger?" asked Alice, wide-eyed.

"Lady," Hawkeye said solemnly, "I have listened to all the sounds of the woods for thirty years. There is no whine of the panther, no whistle of the catbird, nor any noise made by the devilish Huron that can fool me! But neither the Mohicans nor I can explain the cry you just heard. We must leave here."

Duncan pulled the girls to their feet. As they ran to the entrance of the cave, the screeching was heard again, only this time it was louder! Soon, there were so many yells and cries that it seemed as if demons were right outside the cave, waiting for them. Motioning to the girls and Gamut to stay inside, Duncan removed his pistols from their holster.

"Whether the cries are a sign of peace or a signal of war, we must investigate," he said. "Lead the way, good scout."

He and the Huron were perilously close to the edge. . . .

No sooner had Duncan and Hawkeye stepped out from the cave than they were shot at from every direction. The opposite bank of the river flashed with the bright light of rifle fire.

As bullets whistled past them, Chingachgook and Uncas defiantly imitated the shriek of their enemies across the river. Hawkeye quickly raised Killdeer and struck down a Huron in a flash of flame and powder.

The woods once again filled with the loud yells. These too came from every direction, and just as Hawkeye and his companions realized that the Huron were now on their side of the river, four savages sprang from the rocks behind them. Hawkeye held them off, firing Killdeer again and again. When he ran out of gunpowder, he drew out his knife.

"Now, Uncas!" cried the scout. "Take the last of them!"

He had barely uttered the words when a Huron of gigantic height leapt right in front of him. They attacked each other, swinging their knives savagely. For almost a minute they fought, but in the end, the strength of the scout won out. Hawkeye cut the Huron down, and let his body drop to the ground.

In the meantime, Duncan was in a fierce struggle of his own on the cliff above the waterfalls. He and a Huron were perilously close to the edge, each trying to throw the other over the rocks. The Indian grasped Duncan's throat with both hands. Duncan frantically tried to break the Huron's hold when a dark hand and gleaming knife flashed before his face. The Huron's grip around Duncan's neck suddenly loosened, and he tumbled lifelessly over the falls. Duncan gasped for breath, and clasped Uncas's saving arm.

"Back to the cave!" cried Hawkeye. "They aren't done with us yet!"

Chapter Four

"The Huron will try anything to get us!" Hawkeye exclaimed as he, Duncan, Chingachgook, and Uncas scrambled into the cave. Once inside he was met with more bad news.

"I am afraid there is no more powder or shot left," Gamut told Hawkeye.

"Ay," returned the scout, "and soon they will be back like flies on a three-day-dead deer."

Cora got up from the branches where she had been huddled with Alice. "Hawkeye," she said, walking up to him. "You and your friends have been very brave in trying to save us. But we cannot ask you to stay here to be captured or killed. Leave if you want, we will understand." She looked at him beseechingly, and added, "If we come with you, we would only slow you down."

Hawkeye shook his head. "A brave man would rather die a brave man than live as a coward. What would I say to your father? That we deserted you?"

"You must go to him, now. Tell him we need his help," Cora insisted. She walked closer to the scout so she could look him in the eye. "My sister, Gamut, and I are not warriors. The Huron will not hurt us. We are more valuable to them alive, as prisoners."

After a moment's thought, Hawkeye said, "You are right. So listen to me. The Huron will return and you will be captured and they will likely bring you to their village. Break the twigs on the bushes along the way. Once I have more gunpowder, I will find your trail and follow you."

He turned to Duncan. "Struggle with the Indian attackers, but do not kill any of them. If you do, the Huron will seek revenge and slaughter you all. Now, Chingachgook! Uncas! We are off!"

But Uncas did not move. "I will stay," he stated, crossing his arms.

"Uncas, if you stay they will hurt us all," Cora said. "You are noble and courageous, but you must go to my father and tell him his daughters are captives. Go! My prayers are with you."

The young chief gazed at Cora intently, and when he saw how serious she was, he lowered his head and joined with Chingachgook at the river's edge. Together they dropped into the water. The current took them downstream.

"If we hadn't run out of gunpowder," Hawkeye told Cora, "this would never have happened! Be sure that I will have plenty upon my return." Then he too stepped into the water and was washed downstream.

Cora veiled her face in her shawl and drew Alice to her side. They walked with Duncan and Gamut to the deepest part of the cave, and there they huddled together, waiting.

Their wait wasn't long—the Huron, led by Magua, soon found the mouth of the cave. Flashing a ferocious smile of triumph, Magua pulled a tomahawk from his belt. He lifted it above his head, as though daring Duncan or Gamut to attack.

"My brothers call for the life of La Longue Carabine," he declared. "Tell me where he is, and spare your own lives."

"Who do you call 'The Long Rifle'?" Duncan asked. He knew Magua spoke of Hawkeye, but he thought by asking the question, he might delay the search for him.

"You know the one I speak of," Magua spat out. "The white scout who has killed so many Huron."

"He is gone—escaped," Duncan said, drawing the girls close to him as the Huron warriors searched the cave.

Magua watched his warriors, then nodded to Duncan. "Your words do not lie," he said, sliding his tomahawk back into his belt. "So now you will come with me. If we cannot have La Longue Carabine, we will have you instead."

The foursome followed Magua out of the cave and into the night, where the smell of gunpowder still lingered in the air. They walked downriver warily, careful not to anger their captors. Once they were below the falls, Magua pulled a canoe from the bushes and motioned for them to step in. He pushed the canoe from the riverbank while a band of Huron followed on shore with the captured horses: Gamut's mare, Duncan's stallion, and Cora and Alice's Narragansetts.

For mile after mile the canoe traveled downriver. Duncan looked about futilely for Hawkeye and watched for any chance to escape, but saw neither. If he tried to take over the boat, the Huron on shore would shoot him. And he couldn't leap from the canoe and swim, for he couldn't leave the girls behind. So he sat in frustration and watched the band of Indians on the shore walk in step with the canoe.

After many hours, Magua guided the canoe to a clearing on the riverbank and ordered the prisoners out. They then began what seemed to be a never-ending trek through the forest.

Alice quickly grew tired, so Cora alone remembered what Hawkeye had told them—and bent twigs so he could follow their trail. Once, she broke the branch of a large sumach and let her glove fall at the same time. One of the sharp-eyed Huron saw this and snatched up the glove. He then laid his hand on his tomahawk and glared at her. She understood from the menacing look in his eyes that she should not do that again.

Then, she gasped; the Huron was fitting an arrow into his bow. He drew it back and Cora froze. The arrow sprung from the Indian's bow like a lunging snake and flew past Cora's head into the forest. The Indian then ran in the direction of the arrow.

Chapter Five

"You have shot well," Magua said to the Huron warrior when he returned to the path with a fawn slung over his shoulder. The blood was fresh from where he had withdrawn his arrow.

Never before had Cora felt such fear as when the arrow had whisked past her, missing her by the mere width of a hair. Magua watched her pale face curiously.

"We will stop here and eat," Magua ordered. While his men gathered around the small fawn and ripped at its meat, Magua walked over to Cora. She turned away from him, her eyes filled with the disgust that she felt upon seeing the Huron warriors tearing and chewing on the fawn's raw flesh.

"Listen," he said, laying his hand firmly upon Cora's arm. "I was a chief of the Hurons long before the white men came to this land. I was happy! Then the French came to Canada and taught me to drink the firewater. When my Huron brothers and I drank the liquor, we became as stupid as old mules. The white men easily chased us from our lands."

Cora stared into his angry eyes. "What does that have to do with my sister and me?"

"Listen!" Magua repeated. "We became dumb from the firewater and began to follow the white man. The great captain of the palefaces, Colonel Munro, your father, gave us orders and we obeyed. He made a law: If an Indian swallowed the firewater and came into the wigwams of his warriors, that Indian would be punished." Magua was now so close Cora could smell his rancid breath. He continued, "I foolishly drank of the liquor and went into the cabin of Munro."

"I have heard this story," interrupted Cora. "My father is a just man. You broke his command, so he gave you justice."

So he sat in frustration and watched the band of Indians on the shore. . . .

"Justice!" Magua cried, glaring ferociously at her. "I was tied up before all the palefaced warriors and whipped like a dog. See!" he yelled. He tore off his shirt. His back was marked with red and purple scars.

Cora drew back from the ghastliness of the sight. She covered her eyes with her shawl. "I had thought," she said at last, "that an Indian can forgive an injury."

Magua shook his head and spat upon the ground. "Forgive? Hah!"

"Why don't you act like a warrior and fight him instead of stealing his daughters?" Cora persisted, undaunted.

"Why should I risk the muskets of the white man?" returned Magua, with a savage laugh. "As long as you and your sister are my captives, I hold the heart of Munro in my hands."

Cora struggled to reason with him. "At least, release my gentle sister, Alice."

Magua looked at her steadily. He lifted his chin and said, "The girl with light eyes can go back to the gray-headed Munro if you will return with me to my camp and become my wife."

Again the Indian leaned in close. Cora felt she was looking into the eyes of the devil himself. "That will be my justice. Your father will never have a happy day again in his life. He will know that his daughter is the wife of his worst enemy!"

"You . . . you monster!" Cora cried out.

Magua merely smiled. He stepped away from her and called to his men.

The warriors leapt up. One bound the singing-master by the wrists while another two grasped Duncan. The others bent the tops of two saplings to the earth, and tied Duncan by the arms between the branches. Cora and Alice were lashed to the trunk of a tree.

"Hah!" cried Magua, pacing in front of them. "Tell me now, will you become my wife and set your sister free? Or will you die here? It is your choice!"

"No, no, no!" Alice cried out, twisting around to look at her sister. "I would rather die than know you are with that savage."

"Then die!" shouted Magua. He hurled his tomahawk at Alice with such force that it cut the ringlets of her hair before imbedding itself into the tree trunk.

Duncan exploded with anger. In one great effort, he snapped the ropes that held him and lunged at one of the Indians. The two fell into the dirt. Though Duncan was quick, the Huron was stronger. He pressed Duncan to the ground with his knee and drew out his long knife. As Duncan desperately tried to wrestle the knife from the Indian's grasp, he heard the crack of a rifle. The Indian fell back, dead.

The Huron stood aghast at the sound of the rifle crack. Hawkeye leapt from the bushes, swinging his rifle like a club.

"La Longue Carabine!" the Indians yelled as they backed away. But Chingachgook and Uncas were upon them immediately, their knives drawn.

Magua unsheathed his own sharp weapon and with a loud whoop, rushed at Chingachgook. Meanwhile Uncas answered the whoop, and leapt into the fray, cleaving the skulls of his enemies. Duncan got hold of a tomahawk and sent it flying into an Indian charging toward him. Hawkeye lashed out at another Indian as he was springing toward Duncan, knocking him to the ground with the steel barrel of Killdeer.

The struggle ended as quickly as it started, except for the battle between Magua and Chingachgook. The two were on the ground, twisting together like twining serpents in a cloud of dirt. Uncas darted around the cloud in vain, trying to strike his father's foe. But he was unable to distinguish between the two combatants who writhed in the dust. Hawkeye drew back the stock of Killdeer like a club, anxious to strike at Le Renard Subtil.

At long last, Chingachgook gave a powerful thrust with his knife. Magua relinquished his grip, and fell back motionless.

"Strike the finishing blow!" shouted Hawkeye.

In one swift motion, Chingachgook brought his blade up. Just as quickly, he brought it down toward his enemy's chest. But before the knife found its

mark, the wily Huron opened his eyes and rolled from beneath Chingachgook. Taking advantage of the Mohican's surprise, Magua leapt over the edge of the cliff. In a single bound, he disappeared into a thicket of bushes.

Hawkeye grasped Chingachgook's arm. "Let him go," he told the Mohican. "He is only one man, and without any friends, he is like a rattler without fangs. He can do no further mischief for now."

"We're saved," Alice said in a quiet voice as Duncan cut her and her sister free from the tree.

As the sisters embraced, Gamut turned to Hawkeye. "Friend," he said, wiping tears from his eyes, "I thank thee that the hairs of my head still grow where they were first rooted by Divine Providence."

"'Tis nothing," returned the scout. "But come, we must hurry if we are to reach the fort before we run afoul of either the French or Magua again."

No one needed further urging. Cora and Alice gathered the horses, and they set off. With the heat of the day long past, they were able to travel quickly through the cooling forest. As twilight turned to night, Hawkeye halted to consult with the Mohicans. Uncas pointed upward and said, "The moon is full tonight. We will be seen easily by the French if we stay on this path." Chingachgook agreed. "We must also turn the horses loose, their step is too loud." As Duncan removed the bridles and the saddles from the Narragansetts, the girls whispered good-bye and stroked them for the last time. Then the group continued by foot, holding to the shadows.

After a few miles, a heavy, low-lying fog descended upon them. Suddenly Hawkeye started and sprinted ahead. When the others caught up with him, he drew them close, and parted a tangle of thickets.

"Look, the top of Fort William Henry is visible just ahead, at the far edge of the plain," he whispered. "But the forest to our right is filled with the French and their Huron dogs."

The two were on the ground, twisting together like twining serpents in a cloud of dirt.

"It will be difficult to reach the fort unnoticed," Duncan reasoned. "But perhaps in the fog . . ."

"Now you are thinking like a scout!" Hawkeye said cheerfully. "Lead on, my friend."

The fog swirled around them, cloaking their passage across the plain. Before they knew it, the massive wooden doors of Fort William Henry stood before them.

"Father! Father!" Alice cried, flinging herself against them. "It is I! Alice!"

A booming voice rang out from the fort's interior. "Is that my Alice's voice? God has restored my children!" And with a grating of rusty hinges, the doors swung open. Out stepped a tall, broad officer, his hair white with years and service. Colonel Munro wept as he gathered Cora and Alice to his chest. "For this I thank thee, Lord!" he stammered.

Although all the members of the party were happy to be within the walls of Fort William Henry, they soon found out that the fort itself was not safe. Colonel Munro had just learned that he must surrender William Henry because he had too few soldiers to properly defend it, and the additional troops he had been hoping for had been diverted to another battle. The large force of French soldiers and Huron warriors outside could, and would, soon attack and overpower his men. If he surrendered the fort, Colonel Munro and his men would be allowed to leave peacefully.

On the day of surrender, Munro, Duncan, and their guard met the French commander Montcalm on the shores of the nearby lake. Montcalm removed his hat and bowed to Munro in a sign of respect. "To keep the fort is impossible," said the French commander, "it will be destroyed. But you may leave with both your flag and your guns."

With great sorrow, Munro signed the treaty and returned to the fort to prepare his proud men to accept the surrender. Never before had he faced such a dismal task.

Montcalm removed his hat and bowed to Munro in a sign of respect.

Chapter Six

The tenth of August 1757, the day that recorded the abandonment of Fort William Henry, was a sad day for the English. Clouds covered the sun and the shrill sound of the British fifes pierced the chill morning air. The wooden gates of the fort were thrown open and Duncan and Munro marched out. Behind them followed the English soldiers, the sick, the wounded, and the women, including Alice and Cora. At the very end was Gamut, who stayed close to the two sisters to look after them.

Although the borders of the woods were full of Huron, they did nothing to stop the English from departing the fort. Still, Cora and Alice nervously watched the eyes of the warriors as they peered out from behind trees and bushes. When at last the fort was empty and all were crossing the plain, a lone Indian stepped from the forest. He approached a woman and tried to pull her colorful shawl off her shoulders, but she refused to release it. He grasped his tomahawk and struck at the woman. At that moment, Magua rushed from where he had been hiding in the forest, shouting a soul-piercing war whoop.

With that signal, more than two thousand Huron broke from the forest with bloodcurdling yells. With knives and tomahawks raised, they rushed at the English with the force of a bursting dam.

Though the soldiers tried to defend themselves and the women, they were no match for the deadly Huron. Knives tore through uniforms, and tomahawks took the lives of brave English soldiers. The scene was one of confusion as the soldiers tried to form battle lines, but it was no use. Munro sped off to find Montcalm to put an end to this travesty, while Duncan, Hawkeye, and the Mohicans fought on.

The sisters stood horror-stricken as the battle raged around them. Alice's face grew white, and Cora just managed to catch her before she fell to the ground in a faint.

"Lady," Gamut said to Cora, "this is the jubilee of the devils. Only one thing will put them to flight." And to her amazement, he began to sing a hymn in a loud voice.

Indian after Indian raced up to the singer with knife drawn to take his scalp but none did. Whether it was out of curiosity or astonishment, they passed over him to attack other less courageous victims.

Then Magua snuck up from behind. "Come," he said, laying his soiled hands on Cora's dress, "my wigwam awaits you. Is it not better than this place?"

Cora recoiled in horror. "Never! Kill me if you want, but take your hands from me," she cried out. But the Indian had already grabbed hold of Alice, knowing that Cora would never leave her sister. Lifting Alice into his arms, Magua moved swiftly across the plain toward the woods. Cora and Gamut raced after him. Magua placed Alice on the back of one of the Narragansetts he had found wandering in the forest and motioned for Cora to get on. Gamut, refusing to desert the girls, hopped upon the second of the two horses. Magua quickly led them away from the battlefield. The forest closed in around them.

Munro, Duncan, Hawkeye, and the Mohicans fought the Huron through the woods for three bloody days, but eventually were forced to return to the fort because of their small numbers. As they approached, they were stunned to see the fort in ruins, and the field covered with slain soldiers. The French leader Montcalm was nowhere to be found.

Duncan and Munro fell to their knees, but were too exhausted to cry for their massacred comrades and Munro's missing daughters. They could only stare in horror. Uncas returned from the edge of the forest with something in his hand.

"This . . . " he began, holding up a green riding veil.

"Is Alice's!" Munro said wildly. His next words came slowly, "Is she alive?"

"I also found the Huron moccasin tracks that I have seen before," he replied. "She is with Le Renard Subtil." He kneeled down to help Chingachgook make a fire. "Tomorrow, when the sun is out, we will follow their trail and find them."

"That thieving devil!" Hawkeye spit out. "There will never be an end to his evil until Killdeer has spoken to him."

Lifting Alice into his arms, Magua moved swiftly across the plain toward the woods.

Chapter Seven

In the muted morning light before sunrise, Hawkeye and his friends departed from the remains of the fort.

"Walk only upon wood and stone," the scout said as they entered the woods, "for they leave no footprint as grass does. If we are careful, no Huron will follow our trail to the lake."

When at last they reached the water, the men boarded a canoe, careful not to leave the imprint of their shoes on the sandy shore. And just as day dawned, their small vessel entered the narrows of the lake. The water was smooth and the men paddled hard but with little noise. The canoe moved swiftly among the small islands that dotted the lake.

"I see nothing," Duncan said after an hour, "but land and water; and a lovely scene it is."

"The beauty of these wooded inlets can be deceiving," Hawkeye replied. "Any of these islands may hide a band of Indians, ready to spring upon us. Look there!" Hawkeye pointed up ahead.

Duncan squinted through the glare of the sun off the lake, but saw nothing.

"There they are," whispered the scout, "two Huron canoes and smoke. Do you see?"

But before Duncan could answer, the morning's silence was broken by the crack of a rifle. They'd been discovered! Fortunately, the distance between them and the Huron was too great, and the rifle ball merely skipped along the surface of the water and bounced harmlessly off the birch canoe. But several Huron leapt from the shore into their canoes and began to race toward Hawkeye's vessel.

"I'll let Killdeer answer them," Hawkeye said as he set aside his paddle and raised his rifle. Taking careful aim, he pulled the trigger. A thundercrack

"I'll let Killdeer answer them," Hawkeye said as he set aside his paddle and raised his rifle.

boomed across the lake and the Huron in the lead canoe fell backward. The chasing canoes clustered together and stopped their pursuit.

"Row for land," Uncas said, digging his paddle into the water with even more force. "We have the upper hand at the moment."

When they reached shore, they carefully hid their canoe under a pile of brush. Then they took up their rifles and began to search for the Huron trail. Hawkeye urged them to be especially vigilant.

"I have found that their trail normally runs north to Canada," said Hawkeye after several miles of walking. "But the Huron are tricky and rarely leave an imprint on the earth. We must uncover every fallen leaf to see if it hides the marking of a Huron foot."

At that moment, Uncas bounded forward like an excited deer.

"Look here beneath this stream," he said, his eyes bright. He squatted down and raked a mound of dirt across the path of the water, diverting its course. As the bed of the small stream emptied, the print of a moccasin became apparent in the soil.

"'Tis the trail!" exclaimed the scout, clasping Uncas's arm. Chingachgook looked upon his son proudly.

"Hawkeye, you were right," Uncas said, pointing north. "The captives are being taken to Canada."

"With the daughters of an English colonel as his prisoners, his tribe will make him chief," Hawkeye said after some thought. "He will become even more dangerous."

They followed the trail for nearly forty miles through valley, forest, and hill. Their legs ached and they were drenched in sweat. Finally Chingachgook heard a faint nickering, and they soon found the girls' Narragansetts, abandoned. Although there was no sign of the girls or Gamut, Hawkeye said with relief, "Our march has come to an end. We are in the enemy's country."

It was not long before the search party reached a Huron settlement.

Duncan pointed ahead and whispered, "Look ahead, there is a strange-looking Indian on the trail."

"The imp is not Huron," Hawkeye told him as he eyed the figure, "nor of any of the Canada tribes. By the looks of his clothes I would say that he stole them from a white man." Grasping his rifle and bending low, the scout moved quickly and silently toward the curious-looking Indian. As he drew close, he heard the man singing a strange song. Hawkeye straightened up and laughed heartily.

The gawky "Indian" turned. "Might not a man sing a song to the Almighty in the quiet of the forest without finding himself to be the sport of other men?"

"Gamut!" Hawkeye smiled, sitting beside him. The search was over.

Duncan ran to Gamut. "Alice! Where is my gentle Alice?"

"Magua has brought her to the Huron village," Gamut told him.

"And Cora?" Uncas questioned.

"He has put the sister among the Delaware tribe that live nearby," Gamut answered.

"It is a rule of Indian policy to separate captives and flatter one's neighbors by placing one of the captives in their camp," explained Hawkeye to Duncan and Munro. "Magua wishes to make better friends of the Delaware."

Duncan interrupted. "He also knows that in holding Alice, Cora dares not escape. Otherwise her sister will be killed."

Colonel Munro straightened his uniform and asked, "And where is this devil, Magua?"

"Hunting moose with his men," Gamut told him.

Duncan turned to Hawkeye. "Disguise me so that I am not recognized, and I will go into the village and find Alice."

Hawkeye looked at him seriously for a moment before he replied. "It will be risky, but God bless you! You have a spirit as brave as a Mohican."

When Duncan, now with painted face and feathered headdress, and Gamut entered the Indian village, the children laughed at the sight of these two strange-looking men. Their noise brought the warriors from their tents.

Gamut led Duncan past the curious Indians to the tribal council lodge. A flaming torch lit the compound, sending its red glare from face to face and figure to figure.

Duncan entered and walked to the middle of the lodge. Along the walls stood numerous young and strong warriors, eyeing Duncan suspiciously. Upon the floor sat several older Indians. Duncan assumed the one with the largest headdress and red cloak around his shoulders was the chief. After several minutes, the old man spoke.

"Do you speak English or Huron?" he asked.

Duncan had already decided to speak in French. He would claim to be a doctor sent by the French, for the Huron trusted the French.

"Speak!" the chief said again. "From where do you come?"

"I have been sent by the French in Canada to go to the Huron and ask if there are any sick among your people."

"My Canada father does not forget his friends," said the chief, nodding thoughtfully. "I thank him. An evil spirit lives in the wife of one of my young men. Can you cure her?"

Duncan, knowing he had no powers to cure even a common cold, replied, "Some spirits are very strong and are difficult to cure."

"My French brother must be a great healer, for why else would our Canada father send him?" insisted the chief. "He will try?"

Duncan looked around the room. In the shadows to one side stood a short

pole with several human scalps suspended from it. He tried not to stare at them, but he was suddenly too nervous to speak, so he simply nodded "yes." As the chief rose to escort Duncan to the sick woman, a high, shrill yell exploded from outside the lodge. Duncan quickly slipped outside only to see that Magua was returning from the forest with a captive—Uncas!

The chief and Gamut joined Duncan outside, and Duncan, trying not to betray his shock at the sight of Uncas, followed them to the sick woman's tent, which jutted out from the mouth of a cave. "Leave us now," Duncan said to the warriors and the assorted women in the tent. "This singer must begin his song to the spirit." Gamut began to sing a psalm as the Indians filed out of the tent. But as he sang, a dark and mysterious creature entered the area from the dark mouth of the cave that opened into the tent. As it came closer, they saw it was a bear.

The sight so unnerved Gamut that his song faltered. His eyes grew wide as he backed away from the creature.

"Hist," came the sound from the bear. Gamut fumbled for the entrance to the tent, and nearly tripped over himself in his haste to get out.

Now Duncan knew that the Indians quite often captured young bears and tamed them as they grew. He was not nervous until the bear started to lumber toward him. He looked about for a knife or a tomahawk but found none. The bear then sat as a man would and began pawing at its snout. At once the hairy head fell to one side, and in its place appeared Hawkeye's sturdy face.

"Hist!" he said again, warning Duncan to be silent. Hawkeye then told him how he had stolen the costume from the tent of the tribe's magician and had been searching through the back of the cave for Alice.

"Have you seen her anywhere?" Duncan asked.

Hawkeye peered over the walls that divided the large cave into many smaller rooms and pointed. "She is there, by the door," he said.

Upon the floor sat several older Indians.

Duncan leaped through the door and fumbled in the dark until he stood at Alice's side.

"Alice!" he exclaimed, embracing the astonished girl.

"I knew you would never desert me. But we must find Cora! Magua took her to the Delaware," Alice said frantically, pulling at his arm.

Hawkeye stood at the mouth of the cave listening outside. "The hunting patrol has just returned into the village. We must flee."

"What about Gamut?" Duncan asked.

Hawkeye motioned them out. "No doubt he will play the singing fool and the Huron devils will not harm him. Hopefully we can escape before we are noticed." With that they exited the cave and departed, cloaked in the night's darkness.

Once back in the forest, Hawkeye turned to Duncan and Alice. "Follow the river through the valley and it will bring you to the Delaware village. It seems that all the Huron warriors are back in the village so you will not be chased if you hurry. I must first ensure that Munro and the others are alright, and then I'll meet you where the Delaware camp."

"Oh, Hawkeye," Duncan said in despair. "Magua has Uncas—he's somehow captured him. It is too risky for you to return again!"

A shadow passed over the scout's face. "You have risked your life for Alice," he said. "I must now do so for Uncas. He is as close as a brother to me. I have fought at his side many times, and knew that as long as he was alive, no enemy would be at my back. Winters and summers, nights and days, we have traveled the wilderness together. We ate from the same dish, and one slept while the other watched." And here Hawkeye stared straight into Duncan's eyes and spoke with a seriousness that the major had not sensed in the scout before. "There is but a single Ruler of all people, whatever may be the color of the skin; and I call Him to witness. Let it never be said that Hawkeye deserted his friend in a time of need!"

At once the hairy head fell to one side, and in its place appeared Hawkeye's sturdy face.

The scout turned from them and retraced his steps toward the Huron lodges. Duncan drew Alice close as they set out upon the moonlit path along the river that led to the Delaware village.

Hawkeye crept back into the village and put the bear's head back on in case he was seen. He stole through the village, gazing into every hut he passed, looking for his captive friend. At last he came upon a neglected dwelling on the edge of the village. A light was visible through the cracks of the hut's wall.

"Gamut," he called, finding the singer in front of a weak fire.

"What are thou!" demanded Gamut, who for the second time that night saw a bear approach him.

"A man like yourself," replied Hawkeye.

"Can these things be?" Gamut mused, finally recognizing Hawkeye's voice. "Tell me of Alice and Duncan, are they free?"

"They are. They're on their way to the Delaware," replied the scout. "But tell me, where is Uncas?"

"The young man is in bondage, and I fear his death is decreed. I have sought a goodly hymn—"

"No more words," Hawkeye cut him off. "Can you lead me to him?"

The singer brought Hawkeye to a hut that stood alone in the very center of the village. The warriors guarding the hut stood aside for Gamut and Hawkeye, who they thought was the village magician dressed in his bear suit.

"Beware," shouted Gamut, "the conjurer will now blow upon the Mohican dog and take from him his courage!"

The warriors drew back a little from the entrance and motioned for the supposed conjurer to enter. But the bear, instead of obeying, sat down and growled.

Duncan drew Alice close as they set out upon the moonlit path along the river that led to the Delaware village.

Puzzled, the Huron guards circled the bear until Gamut spoke up. "The cunning man is afraid that his breath will blow upon you great warriors, and take away your courage too." The guards looked at each other nervously.

"You must stand farther off," Gamut explained.

Scared of anything that might take their strength, the Huron moved away from the tent. Gamut and Hawkeye entered the lodging and found Uncas within, bound by both hands and feet.

"Cut his bands," the scout told Gamut, which he readily did.

"Hawkeye!" Uncas uttered in a hushed voice, struggling to stand as Gamut slashed away at the rope around his ankles.

"Shhh. The Huron are still outside," Hawkeye warned him.

"We must find a way to escape and make our way to the Delaware," Uncas whispered, massaging his wrists where the rope had cut into him. "The Delaware are the children of my grandfathers."

"You could outrun the Huron all the way to their village, but I could not," Hawkeye said, removing the bear costume. He thrust it at Uncas. "Take this outfit and go."

The two friends looked each other in the eye, until the young Indian spoke. "I will stay to fight with the man my father calls brother."

"Ay, lad," returned Hawkeye, squeezing Uncas's hand. "Huron desert their friends, though a Mohican never would. But I thought I would make the offer."

Then Gamut interrupted them both. "I will stay and take the place of the Mohican who has fought before on my behalf," he declared. "The Huron have not touched me yet, nor will they, I believe. They think me a fool."

Hawkeye readily agreed that this was the safest plan of all, and the three at once began to switch outfits. Once fully dressed in Gamut's clothing, Hawkeye grasped the singer's shoulder and noticed he was trembling.

"Your biggest danger," the scout told him, "will be at the moment when the

Huron find out that they have been deceived. If you are not killed at that moment, then you won't be. At your soonest chance, make your way to the Delaware. But if the Huron do take your scalp, trust that Uncas and I will revenge your death as a friend would."

Gamut thanked him and bid them to leave as he took his place in the corner where the young Mohican had been bound.

Hawkeye and Uncas easily walked past the guards in their disguises. They were swiftly approaching the shelter of the woods when a loud and long cry arose from the lodge where they had just left. The two looked at each other—Gamut had been discovered!

In the next instant wild yells filled the night air from one end of the village to the other. Uncas cast off his costume and together he and Hawkeye dashed into the darkness and safety of the forest.

Chapter Eight

The morning sun rose upon a busy Delaware Indian village where Cora had been joined by Alice and Duncan, who were followed by Uncas, Hawkeye, Chingachgook, Munro, and Gamut, who had slipped away from the Huron in the chaos following the discovery of Uncas's escape. Women were busy preparing the morning meal while children dashed through the streets, chasing each other. Like the Huron, the Delaware had made a pact with the French. But they had kept their hatchets dull and far from the blood of the English. The tribe was known as a peaceful and hard-working people who did not look for trouble.

But on this day, trouble found them when Magua and his Huron warriors walked out of the forest and into their village. A Delaware chief came out of his lodge to greet him.

"The Huron is welcome here," said the Delaware chief, greeting his fellow Indian. "Why has he come to visit with us?"

"Some of our enemies stole into our village last night and took our prisoners. I believe they are here now," Magua said forcefully.

"Our enemies?" asked the chief. "The Delaware have no enemies. It is the Huron's tomahawks that are red with the blood of enemies."

"A paleface and his friends who are now in your camp are spies for the English. What will the French in Canada think when they hear this?" Magua asked, folding his arms across his chest.

"Who is this palefaced spy for the English?" returned the other, slowly looking around.

"La Longue Carabine," Magua declared.

The Delaware men who had gathered around paused when they heard the well-known name. They spoke excitedly amongst themselves. Then a hush came over the entire crowd. Another name was spoken softly, over and over. "Tamenund."

An aged Delaware walked slowly through the gathered group. He had seen more than a century's worth of summers and his back was bent with old age. Young men touched his robe in reverence. The crowd parted to form a lane, and closed around again as he passed.

When he reached Magua, Tamenund closed his eyes as though to gather strength. Though he was very wise, he knew little of the events of the last few days. "Which of my prisoners is the one they call La Longue Carabine?"

At this point the visitors came out of their tents. Cora stood foremost among them, entwining her arms in those of Alice's. Duncan stood by her side; Hawkeye stood in back.

"I am the man," the scout exclaimed. "I was given the name Nathaniel by my white kin, the compliment of Hawkeye from the Delaware, and La Longue Carabine, 'Long Rifle,' from the Iroquois."

"Your name and skills as a scout are well known to my people," Tamenund said in a voice both hoarse and forceful.

"Great chief," Hawkeye began, "I have killed several of Magua's men, better called dogs, and he seeks my scalp and the scalps of these innocent whites you see before you."

Magua's eyes flashed. "These are invaders of our land, and they call us 'dogs'? He is right in saying that I wish the whites as prisoners, but there is also a snake of our own red color who rightfully belongs to me."

"Why?" Tamenund asked.

"He has fought against the French and killed many Huron. The Huron are brothers to the Delaware, and an Indian who kills a Huron, kills a Delaware!" Magua spat out. "Will you let him live if he has killed a Delaware warrior?"

"Where is this man? I want to see him with my own eyes," the great chief said.

The silence that followed this question continued unbroken for many anxious minutes. Then the large crowd opened and shut again, and Uncas walked up to the sage.

"With what language will this prisoner speak to me?" demanded the old chief.

"Like his fathers," Uncas replied, "with the tongue of a Delaware."

"A Delaware!" cried out the sage. "I have lived to see the tribes of the red man scattered like broken herds of deer, but I have never seen a Delaware kill a Delaware." The old man grew so angry that he shouted to Magua, "Take him, he is yours."

The sound of Hurons crying out for revenge filled the air. Cora, who till this moment had been silent, pushed her way through the crowd, and threw herself to her knees in front of Tamenund. "I beg of you, take back your words! There is no braver or more honest man than the one you see before you!" she cried. But the old man brushed her aside.

Among the cries to burn the Mohican alive, and the waving of tomahawks, Uncas alone stood calmly. And as a Huron warrior lunged at him, he stared him in the eye. The warrior drew his knife and cut through Uncas's hunting shirt, tearing it from his body. But before the Huron could wave the shirt in triumph, he stopped and stared.

At once all was quiet.

Upon Uncas's chest was a beautifully tattooed figure of a turtle. Tamenund stepped closer to him, and moved as though to touch the tattoo.

"Who art thou?" he demanded.

"Uncas, the son of Chingachgook!"

"Is Tamenund a boy?" the startled old man mused. "Have I slept a hundred winters? Is this the same Uncas with whom I fought palefaces when we were strong and young?"

Cora . . . threw herself to her knees in front of Tamenund.

Uncas, looking into the old man's perplexed face with the respect of an honest child, replied: "It has been over eighty years since the Uncas you speak of led men into battle. The Uncas you remember, and for whom I am named, died many seasons ago. Indeed, there are no more Mohicans except for Chingachgook and his son."

"It is true—it is true," the sage relented, his voice weighted with sorrow. His smile disappeared as he thought of the history of the Delaware people, who had also been chased from their rivers and lands.

Uncas stepped forward. "Great Tamenund! Hawkeye and I do not deny that we have killed Huron. But we have never killed a Delaware. Magua has lied to you."

Magua sprang toward them in a fury. "Magua is no liar!" he shouted. "Magua is a chief of the Huron! And I demand as my prisoner"—he paused and pointed to Cora—"this woman. I am a chief and my wigwam is empty. She is mine."

"Is this true?" Tamenund asked.

Magua stood boldly, saying nothing.

Cora cried out, but Magua seized her by the arm and drew her to his side.

"Girl, why do you cry?" Tamenund asked. "A great warrior takes you for his wife. Go! The blood of the Huron chief will pass to your children together."

"I would rather die a thousand painful deaths," exclaimed the horror-stricken Cora, "than marry this savage!" She tried to twist from Magua's grasp, but his hold grew only tighter.

Tamenund shut his eyes and waved a hand before his weathered face. "The words of the Delaware are spoken," he said. "Men do not need to speak twice."

Hawkeye, restraining Uncas from attacking Magua, shouted out, "Great sage! You are indeed wise, but tell the Huron that I wish to bargain with him."

"What do you have to bargain with?" asked Tamenund.

"Let every Huron warrior know that this war will not end soon. Every day that it continues is another deadly chance for them to meet me and Killdeer in the woods."

Magua looked keenly at the scout. "Will The Long Rifle give his life for the woman?" he asked nervously.

"I am your prisoner," Hawkeye said simply. He then turned to Uncas and spoke solemnly. "Tell your father I loved him as a brother. As for you, Uncas, I pray that you live long. We shall meet again in the hunting-ground all men go to when they die. Farewell my friend, I give you Killdeer so that you should never fear a Huron in the woods."

Hawkeye again turned and addressed Magua. "Huron, I accept your offer; release the woman."

Magua looked at Cora, and again at Hawkeye, and for an anxious moment, he doubted. Then, casting his cold gray eyes firmly on Cora, he made his choice. "Magua has but one mind. Come!" With that he took Cora and his warriors back into the forest.

Chapter Nine

The Delaware had forgotten the pride they once had as great warriors. But it was awakened by Uncas. He had stood proudly before both the wise Tamenund and the scoundrel Magua and spoke the truth. Words could not express the admiration that the Delaware felt for the young Mohican.

"The Huron have shamed us too long," shouted a Delaware warrior. "Will you lead us into battle?" shouted another. Soon all were shouting the name "Uncas."

"I will lead you," Uncas said, "and I will again make the Delaware a noble people." The tribe cheered and prepared to follow him. Tomahawks were drawn and knives flashed in the morning sun.

Within the hour, the warriors of the village, led by Uncas, marched into the forest with fresh war paint on their faces and sharpened tomahawks in their hands. Hawkeye took a band of twenty men who followed his footsteps so precisely, it seemed the trail of but a single man. The party was scarcely beyond the banks of the river when the woods awoke with the sound of a dozen rifles. A Delaware fell like a wounded deer.

"No time to take cover," Hawkeye yelled over the rifle fire, "Charge!"

The battle began. Though the Huron had surprised them, they had neither the number of men, nor the spirit of the newly empassioned Delaware. The battle soon turned into a rout. Blood spilled on the forest floor as the leaves shook with each rifle shot. The Hurons quickly withdrew into a thicket where they took time to rest and reload.

Hawkeye knew the Huron were not likely to expose themselves again to rifle fire. So upon his signal, his warriors used an old Delaware trick. Each man stepped out and sprinted around the tree they hid behind.

The sight of the forest coming alive with so many bodies enticed the Huron to fire their guns at the swarm. But by the time the flint on their rifles had flashed, the Delaware had returned to their hiding places. The trees of the forest splintered, and the forest shook from the deafening sound, but few of the clever warriors were hit.

This was the opportunity for the Delaware to strike! They leapt in long bounds toward the Huron and were soon fighting in hand-to-hand combat. The battle was fierce but the surprise of the Delaware rush gave Hawkeye's men the upper hand. Then, a rifle crack sounded from behind the Huron line.

"That is Chingachgook's rifle!" roared Hawkeye. "We have them in the front and back!" Chingachgook and Duncan raced forward to help Hawkeye and his men finish the battle. The Huron who did not die fled into the woods. Hawkeye grasped his old friend eagerly. "How did you find us?" he asked.

"I would know the sound of Killdeer from any other rifle in the world," Chingachgook replied. "And where it sounds, I must go." Hawkeye beamed. Duncan reminded them that the woods were still filled with Huron.

"Where is my son?" Chingachgook asked, looking about. Hawkeye, too, scanned the woods.

"There!" he cried, pointing to a clearing in the forest. Uncas was running so quickly he seemed to be flying. Hawkeye looked for the object of his pursuit, and about a thousand yards ahead of Uncas was Magua. Hawkeye and Duncan immediately joined the chase.

Magua and his men raced up the mountain. Uncas bounded from rock to rock after them with little regard for his own life. He followed them into the mouth of a cave, with Hawkeye behind him and Duncan following him. Their eyes had barely time to adjust to the darkness when they saw the flash of something bright exit the other end of the cave.

"'Tis Cora!" cried Duncan, catching a glimpse of the girl's striped dress.

The chase was renewed with a greater passion. Rock fell off the mountain as the men scrambled up its side. Uncas quickly threw down his rifle so that he could climb with both hands. Duncan and Hawkeye were not far behind, but neither could follow as quickly the Mohican's death-defying path along the rocks.

When the Huron paused on a ledge halfway up the mountain to see if their pursuers were still behind them, Cora wrenched herself from Magua's hold. "I will go no farther," she cried, stepping out to the edge of the rocks that overhung a deep fall. "Kill me if you want; I will go no farther."

"Woman," Magua said, "choose: the wigwam or the knife of Le Subtil!"

He drew out his blade and raised it menacingly over Cora, yet he paused. He could not kill her. At that moment a piercing cry was heard from above. They both looked up, and Uncas appeared to be flying down at them from a fearful height to the ledge. Magua recoiled a step, and one of his men, grabbing the chance, plunged his own knife into Cora's chest.

Uncas screamed and Magua sprung like a tiger bent on killing, first on the murdering Huron, then on Uncas. Infuriated, he plunged his knife into Uncas's back. Uncas, grimacing in agony, struggled to rise, but only got to one knee when his strength failed him. Then, with a stern and steady look, he turned to Le Subtil.

Magua knew the young Mohican would kill him if he did not kill the Mohican first. He drove his knife into the Mohican again. Uncas fell back, lifeless. Whirling the bloody knife, the victorious Magua uttered a cry so fierce, so wild, and yet so joyous, that it echoed a thousand feet below to the Delaware in the valley.

"The palefaces are dogs! The Delawares are women! Magua leaves them on the rocks for the crows!" With that he made a wild leap from the ledge, but fell short of his mark. He grabbed onto a cluster of rocks that jutted out from the mountain and his feet had just found a step in the rocks when a shot rang out in the forest. The arms of the Huron relaxed, his hold loosened, and his dark person was seen falling downward. Killdeer had spoken Magua's name at last.

Chapter Ten

The next day the sun rose on a village of heartbreak. Although the battle was fought and won, no shouts of success, no songs of triumph, were heard from the Delaware. For there is no happiness when a great young warrior such as Uncas dies in battle.

Alice was inconsolable. She sobbed for her sister as six Delaware girls flung forest flowers over Cora's body. At Cora's feet sat Munro. Though the old man had seen much death, never had his heart ached as it did now. After a time, Duncan helped the melancholy man to his saddle.

"Our duty here is over; we will depart for England," Munro said, reaching down to grasp Hawkeye's hand. He turned from where his daughter lay and rode out, his shoulders low. Behind him came Duncan who held the weeping Alice, and Gamut followed them. The Christian burial was completed, and all the white men, save for Hawkeye, departed this somber village.

Then Chingachgook was led from his hut. The body of Uncas had been placed in a chair and dressed in the most gorgeous robes, wampum, bracelets, and medals any triumphant warrior could wish for. The warriors sang a song of praise to their fallen brother as they prepared his grave. Their voices were proud, but Chingachgook stood prouder.

When Uncas's body was placed in the earth, Chingachgook spoke with a low but calm voice.

"Why do my brothers mourn?" he addressed the warriors. "Why do my daughters weep? Because a young man has gone to the happy hunting-grounds? Because a chief has filled his years with honor? The Great Spirit has called him away. As for me . . . my race has gone from this land. My son Uncas was the last of a noble people, the last of a tribe that was honorable, brave, and intelligent.

I have no other sons, no wife." Here Chingachgook stopped a moment so that all could appreciate his words. "Now I am alone; the last of the Mohicans."

"No, no," cried Hawkeye, reaching out toward his friend. "No, Chingachgook, not alone. Our colors may be different, but God has given you and me the same path to walk. I have no kin, like you, no people. The lad that so often fought at my side, slept around the same fire in peace, is gone for but awhile. The boy has left us for a time, but great chief, you are not alone."

Chingachgook grasped the hand that the scout had stretched across the fresh earth. These two sturdy woodsmen bowed their heads together while scalding tears fell to their feet, watering the grave of Uncas like drops of falling rain.

Tamenund, the old sage of the Delaware, spoke in the awful stillness of the moment.

"The palefaces are masters of the earth now, and the time of the Indian has not yet come again. My life has been too long. In the morning of my years I saw the sons of my people happy and strong; and yet, before the night has come, I have lived to see the last warrior of the wise race of the Mohicans."

These two sturdy woodsmen bowed their heads together. . . .